GIRAFFE ASKS FOR HELP

by Nyasha Chikowore

illustrated by Janet McDonnell

Magination Press • Washington, DC • American Psychological Association

To my favorite people to ask for help: Mom, Mercy, Tinashe, Dad, Takieya, Chrissy, Donica, Keisha, Jeff, Jordyn, Jianna, Carla, Derrick, Panama, Ingrid, Mobola, Tia, Corte, UMB School Mental Health Program, my Cherry Hill #159 friends, Liz, Tozer, Selena, my cohort, & my supporters at CNMC SCORE— *NC*

For Tanner, who has gotten very good at asking for help but needs it less and less— *JM*

Magination Press ★

American Psychological Association
750 First Street NE
Washington, DC 20002

Magination Press is a registered trademark of the American Psychological Association. Order books here: www.apa.org/pubs/magination, or call 1-800-374-2721.

Book design by Gwen Grafft
Printed by Worzalla, Stevens Point, WI

Library of Congress Cataloging-in-Publication Data

Names: Chikowore, Nyasha, author. | McDonnell, Janet, 1962- illustrator.
Title: Giraffe asks for help / by Nyasha Chikowore ; illustrated by Janet McDonnell.
Description: Washington, DC : Magination Press, e[2019] | "American Psychological Association." | Summary: Clumsy Gary the Giraffe is disappointed that he still cannot reach the top leaves on trees after turning six, but his friends assure him he is not too old to ask for help.
Identifiers: LCCN 2018011912| ISBN 9781433829468 (hardcover) | ISBN 1433829460 (hardcover)
Subjects: | CYAC: Ability—Fiction. | Helpfulness—Fiction. | Friendship—Fiction. | Giraffes—Fiction. | Animals—Fiction.
Classification: LCC PZ7.1.C4983 Gar 2019 | DDC [E]—dc23 LC record available at https://lccn.loc.gov/2018011912

Manufactured in the United States of America
10 9 8 7 6 5 4 3 2 1

"Good morning!"
Gary Giraffe exclaimed as the
sun came up outside his window.

Today was Gary's 6th birthday, which is a big deal for giraffes. He would finally be tall enough to reach the best leaves from the giant acacia trees.

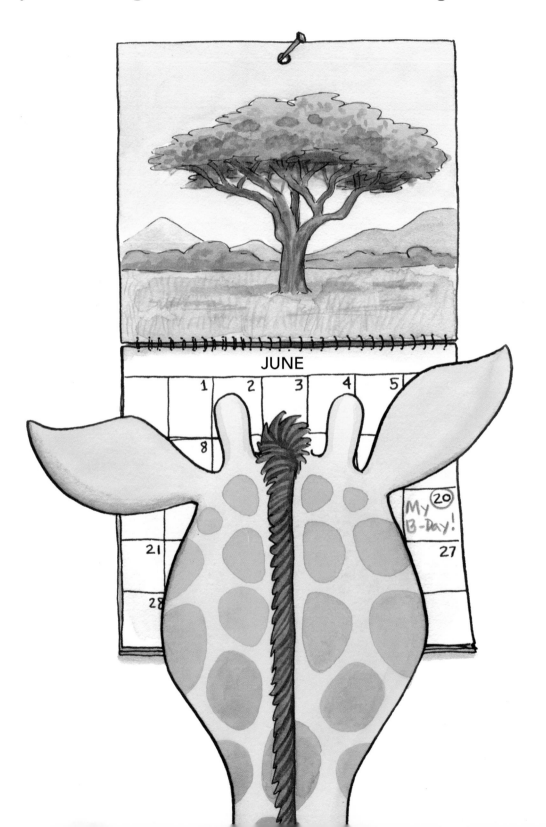

He ran to look in the mirror and saw that his circle and square-shaped spots were getting darker. "Yes! I'm getting older!" Gary yelled with glee.

Gary's dad looked over at him and shook his long neck.
"Gary, your baby sisters are still sleeping.
Can you quiet down? And happy birthday, son!"

"Thanks, Dad!" Gary yelled again. He looked back in the mirror and
stuck out his super long tongue. "I can't wait to get leaves with you!"

Gary's dad shook his neck again.

"Let's go, Gary. The early giraffe gets the good leaves!"

As Gary and his dad walked along, neighborhood animals wished Gary a happy birthday.

Gary had the biggest, widest smile on his face.

Tye Tickbird flew over and landed right on top of Gary's head. "Happy birthday, good friend of mine!" he squawked in Gary's ear.

Tickbirds hang out with giraffes a lot. They eat the bugs off of them and let them know when trouble is near. Tye was Gary's best friend in the whole world.

"Tye! I'm finally going to eat the good leaves today.
I can't wait!" Gary said happily. Tye smiled.
He'd known Gary all of his life, and one thing he knew
for sure was that Gary was super duper clumsy.
He was always stumbling over his skinny legs.

Gary and his dad reached
the acacia tree that
most of the tall giraffes ate
from each day. "Okay Gary,
reach for the greenest,
shiniest leaves you can
find," his dad said.

Gary nervously stepped up towards the tree, tripping a little on his way there. Gary got on his tippy hooves and pushed out his long neck for some scrumptious-looking acacia leaves way at the top.

Closer…closer…

"Ouch!" Gary's dad and Tye said as they covered their eyes.

Gary got up and tried again.
He stuck his long tongue out first,
then pushed his neck up.

PLONK!

This time he fell sideways.

"Okay Gary, that's enough. Let's try
again tomorrow," Gary's dad said.

Gary walked with his head down
the whole way home.

"Better luck next time, Gary!"
Tye screeched, trying to cheer his friend up.

Gary stared out his window at the other giraffes his age eating the leaves from up high with no problem.

"Hmph," Gary said. "If they can do it, why can't I?"

He wouldn't give up! Suddenly, he had an idea. Gary rushed
in and out of the house, gathering up a bucket, a wagon, and a stool.

"This should do the trick," Gary said as he dragged his items back towards the trees. The other giraffes stopped chewing to see what Gary was up to.

He put the wagon down, the stool on top of the wagon, and
the bucket on top of the stool. Gary put his first hoof on
top of the wobbly stool, got the second one up, and then....

Gary came tumbling down.

"HELP!" Tye called
to Gary.

"HELP?" Gary asked.
"Yeah!" Tye said. "When you
can't do something all by
yourself, you ask a friend or
family member to help. HELP!"

"Tye, I'm 6 years old.
I should be able to
reach the leaves alone,"
Gary pouted.

"I'm 10 years old and I still ask my mom and dad for help with hunting!" Chris Cheetah said.

"I ask for help too!" Eli Elephant trumpeted. "Sometimes I need help scratching my back!"

"I'm 30 and I ask my friends for help with my mane!"
Larry Lion roared as he walked up with his pride.

Gary smiled. He really wanted to reach the leaves himself,
but if all those animals could ask for help, he could too!

Gary was excited to test
it out. "Okay, friends!
I need HELP!" said Gary.
He explained how
he kept falling over
when he tried to reach
the good leaves.

Gary, Tye, Chris, Eli, and Larry put their heads together.
"We've got it!" they yelled together.

"We've got it!"

Armed with a plan, Gary and his friends went
straight to the acacia trees. Gary stood under the biggest,
fullest tree he could find. Chris climbed up the tree and
pushed down a branch where the group was standing.

Eli and Larry wrapped a trunk and arms around
Gary's legs to keep him from falling, while Tye
directed Gary to the best leaves.

Gary stretched his neck as far as it would go.

Closer … closer … he got it! They were the
juiciest, sweetest leaves he'd ever tasted!

Cheers rang out from the onlookers.

Gary was full of leaves that night, and the happiest giraffe in town. He now knew that whenever he was in a bind, or stuck in a rut, all he had to do was ask for help.

Note to Parents & Caregivers

Being able to ask for help is an essential skill for everyday life, but one that often has a stigma attached to it. It's natural for young kids to want to "do it themselves," especially when they see adults accomplishing the same tasks without help. Asking for help can sometimes be seen as a sign of weakness or incompetence, especially as we get older. But as we can see in the story, Gary became happier and stronger after recognizing that he didn't have to struggle alone. Help-seeking in children promotes positive psychosocial functioning, competence, and inspires healthy collaboration with the children and adults around them. When children learn to ask for help, not only do they utilize their problem-solving skills, but they also become more adept at communicating and expressing their needs.

The Importance of Help-Seeking

It may seem obvious to us, but asking for help can be a crucial tool to help kids deal with tough problems such as bullying, trouble with school work, conflict with peers, and more. In addition, help-seeking is a skill that can combat many of the risk factors that have been known to cause stress and sadness in kids.

Gary's story is a great way to start the conversation on learning such an important skill. Discussing what asking for help looks like in different settings (e.g. school, home, camp) can help ensure that children can identify adults and peers who are safe and can provide them with the appropriate forms of assistance.

Of course, there's a line between encouraging help-seeking and allowing a child to become dependent on help. Kids should still be encouraged to try things on their own when it is safe and appropriate for them to do so. But being comfortable asking for help when it would be beneficial is a key developmental skill.

What You Can Do

There are many things we can do to encourage help-seeking behaviors in kids. Letting them know that you are there to help them when needed is a good way to make sure they use the skill. Many kids have already been asking you for help since they were toddlers, and it can help to point out what that looked like as they have grown. You may have helped teach them how to walk, helped them with coloring and drawing, or helped them learn how to ride a bicycle. You can also give them examples of when you have had to ask for help in your own life to emphasize that people of all ages sometimes need help.

The following questions can aid parents and teachers in helping children navigate how to ask for help appropriately:

- What are some things you can do without asking for help?
- What are some things you still need help with?
- How can you ask for help?

Have some suggestions ready in case your child needs help coming up with ideas!

Identify Potential Helpers

This can start simply, by asking kids to identify potential helpers at home, at school, and in the neighborhood. This also gives parents a chance to establish clear boundaries for appropriate individuals to approach for help.

A useful activity to promote help-seeking is to introduce children to the individuals you have identified. Parents can take their children to visit neighbors, community members, and family they trust to go over topics that they can help them with. A simple exercise could be to walk over to a trusted neighbor's home and ask for a cup of sugar to bake cookies, or to borrow a rake to gather leaves in the yard. This presents a great opportunity for your child to practice asking for help in a comfortable, low-stakes situation. It also gives you a chance to talk about healthy boundaries afterwards. Although we can ask the neighbor for a cup of sugar, we probably shouldn't also be asking them for the flour, milk, and eggs! We can ask the neighbor to use their rake, but once we are done we have to give it back to them in the same condition we received it.

Knowing who not to ask for help can be equally important, and those boundaries should be clearly established as well. Emphasize that they should only approach and request help from known, trusted adults (or kids!). Many kids may already know this, but it can be helpful to reiterate, especially as we're asking them to brainstorm a list of people that they can approach.

Model Help-Seeking

Help-seeking can be modeled in your home, too! If your child has a sibling, perhaps they can ask for help with picking up toys. You can ask your child to help you with a house chore (e.g. dishes, sweeping, garbage duty), or even something fun, like baking a cake (following up on asking a neighbor for sugar!). It's important to stress that, while of course you can do more things on your own as you get older, no one is ever too old to ask for help. Like we saw in the story, people (or animals!) of all ages sometimes need to ask for help. No one can do everything alone!

Encourage Empathy

Learning to ask for help can also very naturally lead into a conversation about helping others, especially if you're modeling by asking for help, as suggested above. This is a fantastic next step! Not only will your child be learning to ask for help, but they will also be learning how to empathize when you reciprocate. If we go back to the example of asking the neighbor for a cup of sugar, it's useful to discuss that the neighbor can ask us for a cup of sugar in return. We can imagine how it feels to not have enough sugar when baking cookies, and we want to help them. None of us have ever been a short giraffe, but we can empathize with Gary. We can imagine feeling frustrated after not being able to get what we want, too. Empathy is crucial to healthy development, as it helps increase emotional intelligence and is essential to healthy relationship-building with others.

You can encourage your children to empathize and help others in many ways. Sometimes just listening and being a good student can be helpful—it helps teachers give students the information they need in a quiet environment. Encourage your child to think about the class from the teacher's point of view. Empathy can also look like your child sharing a toy or video game with a friend. Letting others have fun with them can show caring and can also give your child an opportunity to help their friend with the activity. Gary's friends empathized with him and not only helped him come up with a plan but execute it as well, which led him to success!

Asking for help is a basic, important skill, but is one that we often don't utilize enough! Encouraging kids at a young age to be independent but also comfortable asking for help sets them up for success down the road.

About the Author

Nyasha Chikowore is a former Licensed Clinical Professional Counselor (LCPC) who has conducted individual, group, and family therapy, and provided classroom and school-wide prevention activities related to mental health. She works to encourage help-seeking behavior in an effort to destigmatize all kinds of help, including mental health services. She is currently pursuing a doctorate in clinical psychology and plans to work with children, adolescents, adults, families, and couples in the near future. She lives in Silver Spring, Maryland.

About the Illustrator

Janet McDonnell is an illustrator and author living in the calm outskirts of the windy city. In addition to illustrating books, magazines, and puzzles, Janet has taught and written for children from preschool to high school. She gets by with a little help from her friends. Visit janetmcdonnell.com

About Magination Press

Magination Press is the children's book imprint of the American Psychological Association, the largest scientific and professional organization representing psychologists in the United States and the largest association of psychologists worldwide.